MW00639973

PETER S. BEAGLE

Return

AN INNKEEPER'S WORLD STORY

Return

AN INNKEEPER'S WORLD STORY

PETER S. BEAGLE

SUBTERRANEAN PRESS 2010

First Edition

ISBN
978-1-59606-309-9

First Edition

Subterranean Press
PO Box 190106
Burton, MI 48519

www.subterraneanpress.com

THE GOOD THING—ALMOST comforting, in a singular way—about not ever being able to shake the Hunters for very long is that you needn't bother trying to outthink them; you can concentrate instead on pure survival. Reaching a sizable clearing, with good sight-lines on all sides, I tethered my mare and sat down on a stump with one leg tucked under me, then unslung the big old bow I really ought to replace and began making a public production of changing the string and studying the exact fletching of my arrows. I hummed as I worked—I think it was Sirit Byar's ballad, "The Juggler," because I always liked that song, but perhaps not. Hard to remember now.

I was deliberately exposing myself, gambling that the Hunters would thereupon credit me with some demonically complex ambush scheme of my own. Any other class of assassin would have responded to this gambit with an arrow—most probably poisoned—slicing out of a thicket to make an end of all my plans and memories together. But I knew the Hunters. They would not attack from hiding: it was not ever in them to have their skills go unrecognized or unacknowledged by their quarry. The only real question, then, was how many seconds I might have in which to react to their reactions. Not for the first time I regretted my inability to learn to throw a tiny dagger like the one my friend Lal always carries in her left boot. I practice, but it doesn't help at all.

The first Hunter simply came stalking across the clearing, hands empty and open, as they most often approach. This was not as I would have had it. I prefer them armed, since anything that clutters and slows those hands in the slightest is my friend.

He smiled warmly at me and purred with what I am sure was genuine affection. "Soukyan, all alone, all unarmed. I can help?" His hands continued to hang at his sides, to all appearances limp, but in fact lethal and pitiless. I paid them no attention, nor did I ever look quite directly into his stone-colored eyes. I was watching his feet.

"I am tired," I said, as simply and flatly as I could make it come out. "There's no beast will not turn at bay at the last, as well you know. Consider me bayed, then."

He laughed outright, a charmingly light and boyish sound. "While you live, danger, danger. Soukyan the betrayer—I know you of old and old." Yet for all his confident air, he was puzzled by my behavior; I could see it in the way his feet kept shifting in small movements that kept them from a firm, constant stance. He asked again, plainly expecting no response, "Cunning Soukyan, what has he in mind?"

I spoke slowly, almost hesitantly, as though the thought were just now forming with the words. "I was just thinking, sitting here—why should the lamb always wait on the wolf's decision? Where have the gods decreed that the hunted may never strike first?"

And with that last word I was *up*, pushing off the leg apparently immobilized by my body's weight, then snapping my half-unstrung bow like a whip. The bit of palmed lead I had squeezed around the endknot worked perfectly, causing the waxed string to curl tightly around the Hunter's neck and catch. I pulled and set him stumbling toward me, desperately off-balance, clawing at his throat, with no hand free to strike out at me. To do him all justice, he almost had the bowstring loose before I broke his neck. I was lowering him gently to the ground when my mare's frightened whinny set me spinning to face the charge of the other one.

And here…here was an unusual thing. The second Hunter was not upon me: he was forty feet away, at the clearing's edge, struggling with the third.

Ah. You do not comprehend. In that moment, no more did I. In truth I would have been less startled by a black sunrise.

I was very young the first time that I faced a pair of Hunters, so soon after taking my leave of *that place*. They were rumors made all too dangerous flesh, and as soon as they were both dead—a Goro slew the first, and I killed the second only by the luck of his arrogance—I blithely assumed that I was free of them and could go my way without forever looking behind me by day, or waking on my feet in the night. What I did not know then was that there is always a third: the leader, moving ever apart from the other two, and more dangerous than both of them together. The exact moment of my education in this regard was personally

Return

memorable, but unimportant. I survived it, a fortune well beyond my deserving: the still-tender spot on the back of my head reminds me yet that the gods must have a certain fond indulgence for ignorant children. And over time I continued to survive, the passages of my life measured by a kind of Hunter clockwork. For while they were not perfect killers, those chuckling little people, they never left your trail until all three were dead; and then, as I discovered, after some time there would be three more following in their tracks, and three more after that, on and on.

But the third stands ever apart, and the second is always more cautious than the first. Through years, nearly decades, it had always been so. Until now. Here in this forest clearing I saw something I could not have imagined, for the third Hunter was clearly *restraining the second*.

It was only for a moment, but unmistakable. Then the second broke free from his fellow's grasp—I saw blood fly from his forearm—and he came for me.

No gentle, smiling assassin, this one, but an animal mad and blind with rage. He came flying and hissing at me, swift as a striking falcon, those deadly hands seemingly gutting the air. I met him with an arrow in each of my own hands, and he was dead before he hit the ground. It had all taken four seconds, at most. From the time I'd first come to my feet, fifteen.

I looked into the eyes of the third Hunter then, seeing nothing at all and having no idea what might possibly come next. He held my gaze for a long moment, then backed three steps into the trees, turned, and was gone.

And I went after him, which was more foolish, and by a far longer chalk, than anything I had done since I was old and experienced enough to know better. Hunters are *hunters*, not fugitives: they find you when it suits their purpose, never yours. You do not plunge off blindly into the woods in pursuit of one— especially not a *third* one, for all sakes' sake. But I had killed two within a quarter of a minute, and I admit I was as drunk with it as a much younger fool would have been.

I will say in my defense that I was aware of, and alarmed by, the ease with which I followed the trail of the third Hunter. I am not the best of trackers—Lal is far better, and the fox is as much her superior as she is mine—but at least I know this, and never imagine otherwise. Yet I was having no least difficulty in my pursuit: there were footprints, torn vines, broken

Return

twigs and branches—everything but signposts every few feet to point the way. Again to do myself justice, I went slowly, fully expecting a strike from every possible direction, including the trees. But for hours there was no sign of the Hunter himself, only of his strange, stumbling passage, until I pushed through a tangle of underbrush and came abruptly upon what looked like his sprawled corpse, face down in the dirt and leaves. I watched for half a dozen breaths and he did not stir, but even so I held my dagger at the ready as I moved towards him.

He was lying on his face, but as I knelt he turned and smiled up at me: not in the sweetly pitiless way that is the last mortal sight so many have ever seen, but with something resembling actual warmth. All Hunters have the same light, eerily cheerful voices, as identical as though they had all been issued them in training, but this voice was heavy with death, which is a sound I know as well as any. He said, "Fitting... fitting it is...wicked Soukyan—turncoat, betrayer. Fitting..."

He coughed, but I saw no blood, nor any wound on him, except for the gash on his forearm, suffered in the fight to restrain the second Hunter from a suicidal attack on me. I replied, "I am no betrayer. I have wished only to live free of *that place,* and have never been allowed that single mercy. So I do what I must, without joy. What plagues you now? I killed your fellows, but I have not touched you." Which was true enough, yet he was certainly dying—it was plain in his smile, as well as his voice. I said, awkwardly, "If you have a message for friends, family, I will see to it," but he laughed then, and I did not go on. As far as I had ever known Hunters had no friends, only each other. He was entirely right to laugh.

But that took the last of his strength, whatever had drained it away so completely. He managed only to mumble, "*The Tree fails...*" I tried to coax more out of him, but what he whispered next I could not hear, and then he was gone. I stayed kneeling beside him for a while.

It took a long time to carry him back to the clearing, and longer still to bury all three of them, even with the soil still soft from recent rains. There are those who wouldn't bother, but life on the run has taught me to clean up after myself; found remains mean more trouble than they are worth, almost always. I said, "Sunlight on your road" to them when I was done. Then I walked back to where my mare was peacefully cropping such yellow summer grass as she could reach, but I did not mount. I had thinking to do, and none of it at all the sort that I favor.

As a general rule, I have never been overly comfortable with unpredictability. Lal's own practice is to expect it in most circumstances; and the fox positively revels in it, since he is always likely to be the least predictable factor in any situation. It may seem odd, given all the patterns of the life I have lived since leaving the strange monastery where I was raised, but like a cat I prefer to know the ground before I put foot to it, to find people where and how I left them, and for them to behave as I am accustomed to have them behaving. Absurd, beyond a doubt—no one needs to tell me that, though those two constantly do—but such is my nature. The notion that a Hunter might go mad and struggle wildly with his superior over a chance to get at me, let alone that that same superior should die at my feet, rather than at my hand, slain by something unknown and muttering mysteriously all the while… none of it *connected*, none of it made any sort of sense. And I need things to make simple bloody sense, which makes me a fool. I know that.

Hunters do not deal in frenzy. Hunters do not ever turn on their own. A Hunter does not simply lie down and cease to breathe, like a poisoned insect. I have been the intimate death of enough of them to know these facts to be inarguable. If it were no longer so—if they who had so tested me were now become as capricious as the rest of this mad world—then everything else I thought I knew had become equally indefinite, and every certainty well worth reconsidering. In which case...

...in which case, returning to *that place*—as I called it even when I lived there—was unavoidable. All that I had just experienced must surely signify *something*. I had to know what it was—and only those who had so long ago been my masters and companions, and later my spurned and murderous enemies, would be able to tell me. I was simply going to have to persuade them to do so without dying in the process.

And I knew I would have to go alone. I do not have so many friends that I can afford to waste any.

Here, circumstance was my ally. Lal had made me swear never to return to *that place* without her and her swordcane, but both of us had shortly after been swept up into separate employments. I had been deep in the north, just short of the Barrens, a long way from the dark woods and swift, cold rivers of my own country, as bodyguard for a wealthy merchant whose fear of assassination extended, justifiably, to very nearly his entire family; consequently I had not seen Lal for almost three years—rumor had her aboard a merchant coaster in the pirate-ridden Straits of Mashaq. As for the fox, who came and went as he chose, he was off on some devious enterprise of his own, which I would walk as far to ignore as he would to keep it from me. With luck my business would be over, for good or ill, before he sought my company again.

I have called it a monastery, *that place,* for lack of a better word; and in a literal sense the term is perfectly accurate. They do indeed have monks sworn to certain oaths and obediences, and there is a distant, unchanging hierarchy of masters whom my eleven-year-old runaway self had regarded as guests and companions of the gods, if not quite gods themselves. But the ecclesiastical aspect is the very least of what *that place* was. When it falls at last to ruin and abandon, as it someday will, that debris will still echo with secrets. For secrets, above everything, are the stock in trade of that silken, shadowed fortress where I spent nearly twenty years of my life. They peep from the cracks in the walls; they scuttle in the corners, and shelter in the whisper of the monks' robes. In my time there, as I learned, there was literally nothing that kings sought to hide, that queens prayed to forget, or the wiliest of officials, church powers and businessmen worked to disguise, that was not known in *that place.*

I was a boy when I first came there, younger than my age in many ways. I left it—running once more—on the same night that I was finally offered entrance into that hierarchy: not as a monk, but as an initiate, a secret-sharer with a wearisome climb through the ranks ahead of me, but with a possibility of such eventual influence as no peasant-born child like me could have dreamt. Somehow I had judgment enough to turn the proposal down, and to fly for my life less than an hour after its making. The Hunters followed.

To return would be a long journey, and I was grateful to have had money enough for once to bargain for my good young mare, rather than the usual hairy, blunt-fanged *churfa;* you cannot imagine the pure restfulness of it, especially over such distance as I now contemplated. You do get used to a *churfa*'s stink and the pacing gait, I will admit, but never to the screaming. And I had no desire to announce my arrival earlier than I had to.

As for provisioning I needed no more than my bow, my flint and steel, a little dried meat, and the *trimoira* dagger, sharp as a winter breath, that I had removed from a lady who took rejection poorly. I am

Return

not especially adept with either points or edges, but I
thought the dagger might come in useful at least for
cooking. Neither Lal nor I travel heavily armed: my
experience is that if you need a wagonload of weap-
onry to feel secure, you are likely doomed before your
bespoke sword clears the scabbard. Good sense, steady
nerves, and a healthy lack of pride will carry you a
deal further.

I had no plan—no strategy at all. I mention
this because Lal, to this day, remains obsessed with
the notion that I invariably set off blindly into the
unknown, improvising as I go, which is simply not
true. But in this case, my reasoning ran, two decades
of plotting and speculating and reasoning had brought
me no closer to ridding myself of the Hunters, nor of
that place's lingering hold on me. Therefore I would see
what proximity would do. My idea was to approach
boldly and innocently, in the guise of a benighted
traveler: a tall, brown woman whom I had not been
in very many years. Not since Corcorua, really, not
since the inn, the old Gaff and Slasher, and the wizard
Lal always called *my friend* and I *the man who laughs,*
who taught me the trick...not since that time had I
again needed to be that woman. However altered or
reduced *that place* might or might not be, it was still

the dwelling of certain persons of great power and consequence. Soukyan the hunted would surely never get within two days' ride of that wicked old house— but a stranger, lost and confused in strange country?

Originally I had been traveling south on the coast road, on my way to another chance of body-guarding in Sai'surak, whose sole attraction was the prospect of a warm winter. When I became aware of the Hunters trailing me, I had turned west—just before Leishai, it was—and now, after our encounter, I went southwest on farmcart roads and goat paths, doing all I knew to avoid notice. I did not know the names of any of the hamlets through which I slipped between midnight and dawn; nor did I recognize any of the songs I heard ploughboys whistling behind their red oxen. Often I could have used the fox's yap-pingly derisive company, or even one of Lal's endless, tuneless chants from her homeland. Yet I stayed alert as I rode, nor ever slept straight through a night, but took my rest in fragments and splinters, for it was hard to believe that the disappearance of three Hunters at once would not have set the shadows in *that place* ringing like temple bells. I raided orchards and kitchen gardens at midnight, killed whatever I could cook over the small, smokeless fires that my sister taught me to make, slept in the saddle from time to time, and rode on.

When I judged the moon and stars to be just so— *the man who laughs'* directions could be maddeningly casual—I said the spell as I remembered it, and let the woman-guise drift down over me, like a cobweb, letting it happen slowly, so as not to bewilder or frighten my mare. In each pool or stream where we halted to drink, I glimpsed the brown face that was not my own more and more clearly, feeling her presence more and more in my body: an old friend come to call, shy with years at the first, but increasingly at ease to find herself welcome. *Hello, old friend.*

Her name in the old days had been Nyatenari; it would not serve me now. I must choose another.

Aye, it was tedious journeying, that long road that I plodded back into the past. The further southwest I struck, the more my path was haunted, not by anxiety over my destination, but by steadily intensifying recollections of a boy running in darkness, his chest splitting with pain, his heart hammering with triumph and terror, weeping for his sister and listening for the dogs. I remembered too well.

As I also remembered—rising before me out of the dank mists, like a dark moon, invisible a moment earlier—the walls and spire of *that place,* with one light showing in the kitchen. Whatever the memory of that solitary light signified for me today, that running boy had never been as overpowered with joy to see anyone or anything. He had burst through the kitchen door, wet with tears, soaked through with sweat and a dead man's blood, and the cook took him in.

As she hid him again twenty years later, when it was worth her life to do so. I have never forgotten her, either.

Far west of Leishai the country turns gradually boggy, especially as you near *that place.* There are marshes fed by underground springs, and there are even occasional patches of quicksand—not deep or wide enough yet to qualify as a dangerous mire, but larger than I remembered, here and there even interrupting the road. I found myself musing on the fact that my former masters and mentors had allowed this path to their dwelling to go so notably to ruin. I had to assume, for safety's sake, that the change was one of deliberate policy, but I had other hopes I couldn't ignore.

A mile or so from my goal I dismounted, caught up the mare's reins, and walked on with her the rest of the way: not because I had any expectation of arriving unobserved, but because she had kept her end of the

Return

bargain faithfully, despite lately favoring her off hind leg somewhat. I intended to ride away as I had come; my life and death might very well hang upon her good health.

That place always takes you by surprise. It appears abruptly between one bend in the road and another—not loomingly sky-filling, like the black castle in Fors na'Shachim, where the Queens live, nor as slyly terrifying as the Nameless Tower just west of Drakali, which is supposed to be empty and is not—but oddly elegant, even attractive, with its two simple wings, two soapbubble roofs, and single spire. I knew a house once that was not really a house, and ate things. *That place* is a little like that.

My strongest impulse was to enter by the half-hidden kitchen door, as I had first come there, and later left; and I probably would have done so, had I imagined that my childhood friend and savior the cook might still be behind it. But I knew better, and could only pray that she had suffered no punishment for aiding me. When I stabled the mare I saw several other horses in residence, so I knew *that place* was not yet abandoned; then I walked around to the great double front door—which has no lock, and needs none—and pulled the bell rope.

Standing once again on that stone threshold, I was prey to a chill loneliness that made me wish I had listened to Lal's fiercely urgent warnings. What had I imagined accomplishing on my own? What exactly did I *want* to accomplish, with or without assistance? To strike at the Hunters, or at the Hunters' masters, when I had no idea how many of either there might be, but a very good idea of the damage that even one Hunter could wreak on a human body? To pull down *that place* against the wishes of the great figures its masters could call on to extend a finger and crush me, if they could not be bothered to do it themselves? Oh, I heard Lal in that moment, as clearly as ever I have.

I assumed that I had been intently observed on my road for at least this day, and was being watched now, but I had already determined to behave like any traveler innocently requesting shelter from a house of humble clerics. I rang a second time, stepped back and called out loudly, "Good fathers, I have lost my way and seek lodging for the night—can you oblige me?" The bell woke no echoes, nor could I hear it sounding anywhere within, but I knew where it rang, and who heard it, and I knew who would be most likely to answer the door, as long a time as it had been.

Return

I even knocked once or twice, loudly and pointlessly, just because he always hated that.

As I had expected, it was Brother Laska who opened to me. Brother Laska had been doddering through my youth; he was doddering and palsied now, hanging onto the great door to stand erect, seemingly barely capable of speaking a coherent sentence of challenge or welcome. Nevertheless, he remained as ominous and chillingly senile a figure as I remembered, and I would have wagered whatever I possessed that he continued in *that place's* highest council, glowering and hiccupping as ever before. I greeted him as a stranger, giving him the name I had decided upon—Jalsa—and saying "Father, I am a woman alone and unprotected, with my horse spent and night coming on. I beseech refuge and asylum therefore." Then I held my breath, strangely assured that if Brother Laska did not know me in my woman's guise, nobody would.

Nor did he; but merely blinked his yellow-crusted eyes, muttered something indistinguishable from the chronic whine in his chest, and turned, leaving the door open, to totter up the stairs and deliver my message. Seeing no reason to wait outside in the growing dark, I walked into the house behind him, where I stood very still indeed, looking around.

Nothing, and too much, had changed. As far as I could judge, not a single item in the grand entrance hall had been moved or replaced, cleaned or repaired. As a back-country peasant child I had never ceased to marvel at the style and furnishing of the great house that had given me such safe haven: it was only now—grown, traveled and far more questioning—that I noted the worn weariness of chairs and benches, carpets and curtains and such ornamentation as there was. The stone elegance of the exterior was matched nowhere within: what was not dark oak was heavy cast iron or dull brass. No one would ever have taken that dusty, lifeless mansion for a fortress of silence, a stronghold of secrets.

The man who came down to meet me I had once known as the young Brother Caldrea, firm overseer of those even younger, like me; but by his bearing and his confident air I realized immediately that he had clearly been promoted. And there is only one rank above "Brother" in *that place*.

He was as lean as I remembered, and rather slight, not yet fifty, with thinning blond hair, a well-cut blond beard, eyes of an oddly opaque gray, and pale skin drawn notably tight over strong jaw and cheekbones. He wore a robe no different from Brother Laska's robe, except for a very small golden pin in the shape of a circle up near his throat. He raised an eyebrow at the sight of my bow, but addressed me genially enough, saying, "Madame Jalsa, you are safe here with us for the night. I myself will show you to your room."

I did not show in any way that I knew him, or the house. Instead I thanked him for his charity and his kindness, and I followed him along the right wing of the house, to one of the windowless cells kept for visitors, which was, as they all were, bare and clean and cold, furnished only with a rope mattress, a basin, and a bucket for necessities. A servant I did not recognize brought hot water, and Master Caldrea departed courteously, saying that as a woman I would not be permitted to dine in the refectory, but that he would be pleased to serve me in his own quarters, at my convenience. Should we say at seven of the clock?

He left me all but speechless, and even warier than I had come. To begin with, masters, abbots, priors and the like, even in as dubious a cloister as this one, do not solicit women's companionship at meals, let alone meals taken in such suspicious intimacy. Second, I had serious doubts that my small enchantment would survive a full evening of Master Caldrea's probing company—I remembered him ruthlessly quizzing novices regarding their midnight activities until he invariably evoked tearful confessions of every sort. Thirdly...thirdly, I had probing to do myself, concerning the origin and nature of the Hunters, and I was not at all certain that I possessed either the deviousness or the patience to find out from Master Caldrea what I needed to know. I missed the fox: in his human form he could have done it while methodically devouring everything set before him, and before our host as well. I dislike a number of things about the fox, but his value to me over our years together very nearly matches the estimate he himself places on it.

I slept out the rest of the day on that sagging, prickly rope mattress; then rose, an hour or so before mealtime, to clean myself up as best I could, and to dig a few remotely passable clothes out of my saddlebags. I had no feminine garments with me when I changed my course to come here, but those who get their living at perhaps one remove from a highwayman will still carry a sewing kit when they have thrown away the useless sword. A cautious slash *here*, a judicious stitch and tuck *there*, made by firelight and the odd thoughtful sunrise, and I had become acceptably equipped. By fashion, at least, Master Caldrea would not know me from his own maiden aunt.

The stairways and corridors of *that place* are crowded with whispers: you can go days there seeing only servants and silent monks, yet feel yourself continually eavesdropping on a dozen muttered conversations, all happening almost out of earshot, in different times, to different ends. I passed half a dozen brothers on the stairs as I set off, slipping by silently, nodding solemnly to me under their gray cowls; but I met others as well, others who, without exception, covered or averted their faces when they passed me, as though I were being shunned. I knew several all the same, despite their feeble incognito, and it was clear that *that place,* however tempered—I could not help but note a distinct decline in the cleanliness of the halls and the manners of the help—was still functioning as it always had: as a clearing-house or meeting ground for every kind of treacherous plot and betrayal. And I hid my own face as best I could, because I knew the price of knowing. I had seen it paid here more than once, when I was still young.

Master Caldrea's apartments were, surprisingly, not set apart at the top of the house, as I remembered the previous Master's rooms, but shared the second floor with the bare cells of the senior brothers, for whom I had once fetched and carried, run errands, and trudged back and forth with messages to deliver. Now I was a guest where I had long served, and must needs keep such old memories from betraying my disguise. Consequently I went out of my way to lose my way, so to speak, and made sure to require escort to Master Caldrea's door. I arrived appropriately late, and he apologized graciously for not having thought to send a servant.

His quarters were hardly less austere than those of its neighbors, being only somewhat more spacious and having a large window, with—as it happened—a view toward the marshes, through which I had made my escape so long ago. The dinner, however, lent final credence to the servants' old belief that certain people dined quite differently from the rest of us. Indeed, it occurs to me now that those years spent downstairs watching steaming covered dishes go upstairs gave me something of a taste for hunger, and my host remarked on it, though not in those words. "Either you are displeased by the meal, which distresses me, or else you believe, as I do, that one should never feed full, but always leave the table wanting a bit more. Wanting, but not taking."

"This is so," I agreed. "The food itself is delicious beyond description—I've never enjoyed finer *kashin-tao,* or even suspected that the Southwest could produce such a delicate white *branetz*—"

"The very first pressing. Pass this way again, and it will be richer, more mature." He tucked his bent right-hand fingers into his left palm, squeezing and releasing: a nervous habit that I did not remember from before. "But *will* you visit a second time, there's the question? I sense a certain purpose in your presence, Madame Jalsa, for all your protestations of going astray on the road. Am I mistaken in this?"

"Entirely, entirely," I assured him, laughing. "Such purpose as I have takes me to Lantry na'Dals, where a niece of mine has fallen ill, and needs me to help care for her children for a time. But my attendant and I became separated—stupid, stupid man, this time I really *will* discharge him—and had it not been for discovering your establishment, I'd have surely slept cold on hard ground tonight. Thank you, Master."

"Our good fortune." He poured us both a bit more of the *branetz,* and raised his glass. "To bungling attendants!" We drank, and he went on, "But you must know that you are nowhere near Lantry. If you started at dawn tomorrow, you would not reach it by nightfall—it will be a full day and a half, at the very least, before you see your niece and her children." He raised an eyebrow and clucked his tongue softly.

Return

I said meekly, "There is a road just past Malcourek—a straight road, much shorter, but old and long overgrown, easy to miss, as we plainly did. I would appreciate any counsel you may give me tomorrow."

"And you shall have it," Master Caldrea assured me heartily. "But by your leave, bear with me for a single moment further. You yourself have never been here before that I am aware of—I certainly see nothing obviously familiar about you—yet why is it that I seem to *feel* something that I should know...that I *do* know, and cannot quite put my hand on. Can you tell me what it might possibly be, this something? Consider your answer for a moment, Madame Jalsa, if you would be so good."

There was nothing threatening in the last words themselves, but the sudden warmth of his smile unnerved me just a trifle, even as I knew that the time had finally come to take my next step in this dangerous game. After a mere few hours in this endlessly deceptive place, a larger lie than a simple disguise had already taken hold of me, taken root.

"I can," I said. "There *is* a connection—one I should have spoken of directly I arrived. I ask your pardon." Master Caldrea continued smiling. I drew a long breath and said, "Soukyan."

Having spoken his name—my name—I let a useful tension animate my face, and waited. "Well," Master Caldrea said presently. "Soukyan." "I *am* on the road to Lantry na'Dals. That was not deception. But I have no attendant, and I did not come to your door first by mistake." "You should indeed have told me honestly that you were here in search of him. And I would be entitled to regard it as a breach of hospitality that you did not." The smile was gone, but he did not seem indignant; only thoughtful. "Master, he wronged me and my family past enduring!" I put all the earnestness I could summon into my voice. "He came to you with my poor brother's blood smoking on his hands, and when it was found where he had fled for sanctuary, we naturally gave up all hope of justice—of vengeance—and could only leave him in your hands and trust to your well-known mystical wisdom." *Careful now—he was never vulnerable to flattery.* I lowered my tone and went on. "The pain he caused, the damage he did—to all the family, all of us—it hardly bears recounting. Our mother was dead within a month of my brother's death. My own marriage failed to survive, so unsympathetic was my husband to our loss, and each of us could tell you similar tales. The family business died with my brother, leaving us all struggling to survive without him, as we struggle on still." I paused to catch my breath. "We are past an end, Master. I have a right to know—will you give our murderer to me?"

A single glance at Master Caldrea, and I knew that I had caught him fairly amidships. He went on studying me, still without his earlier geniality, but equally—as far as I could tell—without any suspicion. At length he said, "Soukyan has...left us, madame."

I endeavored to appear stunned, frustrated and further resolved all at once. I said, "May I know where he has gone? I ask for others, not myself alone."

"No, you misunderstand," Master Caldrea said. His right-hand fingernails were digging harder into his left palm. "Soukyan is dead."

Even when you know better than anyone else in the room why something cannot be so—and when you know just as well that the person lying to you knows the truth—even then, it is a remarkably disorienting experience to be informed that you are dead. I admit that I did not altogether have to pretend shock at Master Caldrea's words. I said in very nearly genuine astonishment, "Dead? *Soukyan?* How...how long?"

"Oh, quite a few years now." Master Caldrea made something of a show of casual reflection. "He left us most abruptly—flying out as he flew in, you might say. There was some trouble, of a sort you need not concern yourself with, and it became necessary to..." He shrugged, hesitating. "There really was no choice, in all honesty."

"The Hunters," I said. "You sent the Hunters after him."

This time it was Master Caldrea's turn to attempt to conceal surprise, and fail. I laughed briefly. I said, "Master, I live far from this place, and have never visited here before. Yet even *I* know that there are such creatures, if I know no more than that. Who the Hunters are, *what* they are, what services they perform—what they are to you and your companions—all this is utter mystery, and may remain so, for all of me. But they do not walk in the world and leave *no* trace of their passage. Tongues wag." I fell silent, as we stared at each other over the last of the wine, and then I added, "What you choose to tell me—about the Hunters, or about *him*—over that, I have no control. But on my family's loss I believe I do have a right. Thank you for your hospitality, and the excellent dinner." I stood up to leave.

Return

With no reply, with no more than the flick of a forefinger, he sat me down again before I was aware that I was sitting. And that was the first time I understood fully how the Brother Caldrea of my childhood had become the Master. He said, "Dear Madame Jalsa, I could not possibly allow you to leave under such a misapprehension. The Hunters are not hired killers—assassins on retainer, as it were—but just as much a part of this house as I am." He chose a *sulyak* pear from a bowl on a sideboard, offered it to me; and, when I shook my head, began to peel it with a delicate silver penknife as he continued. "As I think you are obviously aware, there is a further aspect to this house that is not entirely of the cloister. We are not all monkish here, not all devoted to contemplation of the Infinite. We are more of the mundane world than we may seem, and there are those of us who—ah—choose to take some little part in its workings. That is why..."

"That is why Soukyan is dead," I finished for him, "and not at the justified hands of the family he destroyed. Well, there is no more to be said, then—I have a dawn journey ahead of me," and I rose a second time, feeling as though I had been breathing shallowly for hours. Master Caldrea summoned a servant to escort me back to my room, and walked with me to his own door, promising to have me set on the right road in the morning. I said, "I thank you, but I know the way. And I do not wish to trouble anyone here further with my disappointment."

Nibbling the hard little pear at the door—he had summoned a servant to escort me back to my own room—he shook his head, saying, "I regret that we will not meet again, but there will be a proper breakfast waiting for you before you depart, and your horse will have been fed and groomed as well. And so farewell, and a comforting slumber to you, Madame Jalsa."

Back in my room, I lay down on the rope mattress and forced my eyes to close, knowing how much in need of rest and sleep I was. But all I could feel was the same saturating terror that had overwhelmed me on my last night in this house: exactly the same sense that I had no more than an hour to live, and that no one would learn whom I had been, nor what had become of me. Of my own choice, I had returned to a place whose walls were shadow: shadows that had weight and movement and bad intent, shadows that concealed beasts of evil, empty knowledge. Shadows that meant to crush me into shadow. *This was a mistake. I am not strong enough for what must come next. I have no business here.*

Return

I gave myself that hour on the bed, and then I rose and went down the stairs. At the door I paused in the darkness for one last long look at the place that had saved me and lost me and marked me forever; and what went through my mind cannot be described more clearly than that. I had my hand on the inner latch when a wheezing, roupy voice I knew as well as my own said behind me, "You take leave of us early, lady."

I turned to face the yellow-white hair emerging from a closet under the stair, where rumor had always had it that he slept to foil apprentices trying to slip out by night. Brother Laska was as I had always known him: gaping and squinting wet-mouthed, peering at me as though through a Cape Dylee fog, with his head thrust forward like a turtle, and his eyes as far beyond any recognizable color as his voice was beyond tone or expression. Nevertheless, he addressed me directly, saying, "I know why you come here. I know what you seek." A deep, raking rasp in his chest; a brief, ugly coughing spasm. "I can take you there."

Laska? What in the world could Laska, practically born senile, know of any mission of mine? I kept my voice sharp, irritated as the woman I was impersonating would have been with a servant's disrespect. "Fellow, you will take me nowhere but to the stable and my horse. Be quick about it, and silent, lest I rouse the Master." Lal does that sort of thing much better than I.

Laska made a sound I had never heard from him before: a sort of hawking sigh that I realized, after a moment or two, was meant as laughter. He said, "The Tree."

I stood as still as I ever have in my life, including the time when I hid from the Hunters in a manure wagon with the fox. Laska laughed again. The sound was not as chilling as the two words, nor the words nearly as frightening as the notion of Laska laughing at all. He smiled at me with his raw gums and his half-dozen brown teeth. "The Tree," he repeated. "You have come for their Tree."

I gaped at him, no less amazed than I would have been if my horse had begun to express opinions. He had already spoken more words than I could remember him uttering in all the years I had known him as doorkeeper for *that place*. I said, very cautiously, "Tree? I came for Soukyan, as your Master now knows. But Soukyan is dead, and there is no hope here for me or my family."

A terrible, triumphant smile spilled over Laska's face, spreading like some sort of infection. "Of course, lady. As you say. I will take you to the stable."

Return

It was grimly, darkly fascinating, even for me. Whether or not he had penetrated my disguise—and I could not be certain either way, nor imagine what it might mean to him if he had—in any case, he *knew* there was something disguised somewhere. And if he knew, then certainly my attempt to gull his Master had not survived first trial, and I was right to leave immediately. I could trust nothing here, take nothing for granted—except for the certain conviction that I had done myself no service by this visit, but only armed and alerted my enemies. Something else not to tell the fox, if I survived to see him again. Or Lal, either. Oh, especially Lal.

I said nothing as I followed Laska down the path that led to the stable, even as I contemplated and rejected alternatives. The night was moonless; if the stable proved unattended, I could have the old man unconscious and over the back of my mare in a silent instant, and prod him with questions about the Tree—whatever it was—at a safer distance. Worth the considering.

They were good: not just for monks, but for professionals of any sort. They waited until we were nearly to my mare before they rose silently from the hay bales all around me, even dropping from the rafters like spiders. My bow and dagger were only an arm's length away; but crowded and pinioned as I was—snared by the press of robed bodies, more than anything else—I never reached for them, having no wish to kill any but Hunters.

The look on Laska's face surprised me greatly: there was no triumph of treachery there, but only distress and disappointment. Whoever had arranged for my capture, clearly he wasn't a part of it. I could find no one else to blame but myself, over and over.

They brought me back to the mansion quite courteously, allowing me to walk on my own, but with my arms bound. I passed the rest of the night in the same visitor's cell given to me by Master Caldrea when I first arrived. The only difference this second time was the guard on the door, and the confiscation of my bow, my arrows, and of course the *trimoira* dagger. Considering the circumstances (not to mention that martyr's mattress)—I slept surprisingly well, and did not wake until a young novice brought me an excellent breakfast. I was clearly still Jalsa to him: he blushed carmine and rushed away as soon as he handed me tray and utensils. I ate slowly, paced the little room for a time, exercised as I could, and was sitting on the bed attempting to meditate, when I heard soft footsteps outside, and in a moment Master Caldrea entered alone. He closed the door behind him, and stood with his back to it, studying me.

"Good morning," I said. "You were quite right about the breakfast they serve here—I can't remember a better one. Please pass my appreciation on to the cook."

"I will do that," Master Caldrea replied. "Praise from Soukyan is praise indeed."

He smiled at me, and kept smiling, as I looked down at my woman's body, unable to see any sign that my enchantment had dissolved. "No, have no fear— you are still the gracious and winning Madame Jalsa, as far as human eyes are concerned. But you may as well let the mask fall, don't you think? It will serve you no further, I promise, and I would be greatly pleased to see young Soukyan in his own person again. I really was fond of the rascal, you know." His voice was pensive, curiously regretful. "Speaking for myself, I privately respected his flight from what we offered him, and could not help applauding his success in avoiding so many trackers for so many years. You have all my admiration, my friend." He bowed his head briefly over his clasped hands.

"You knew," I said. "From the beginning?"

43

Master Caldrea smiled, a bit smugly, as he had every right to do. "Do you imagine yourself to be the first who has ever come here behind another face? Never underestimate the power of an old house, Soukyan. It was the house itself that recognized you—it was the house that told me who you were, before ever I came downstairs to greet you. The house knows its own." He chuckled softly. "Actually, the house was quite pleased to see you. I think it has rather missed you, all these years."

The Jalsa-spell barely brushed my face as it slipped away as lightly as it had come. Master Caldrea regarded me thoughtfully, shaking his head very slightly. "Ah, they have been hard years, have they not?"

"I was an ugly baby," I said.

Master Caldrea smiled. "I was not speaking of features, but of expressions. Man or woman, your eyes betray your life. Had you remained with us..." He did not finish.

I said, "Had I accepted, I would have been like you. I'd have spent my life trafficking in pathetic secrets and fears, blackmail and lies and meaningless mysteries. It was not for me, none of it."

His smile hardened. "What was not for you was power. Not because you did not want it—oh, I do remember you, Soukyan—but because you wanted it too much, and you knew you did. In that sense, you were quite wise to run off—I only marvel that you dared to return, and in such a manner." He paused, cocking his head. "Would you care to tell me your reason?"

"I came to destroy the Hunters," I said. "I am tired of them, and it is time for them all to be gone. That is my reason."

It should tell you something important about Master Caldrea that he neither laughed outright, nor gave any indication that he was doing so inwardly. Rather, he nodded slowly, as though I had confirmed a pet speculation of his, and responded after a moment, "How fortunate that you should have chosen just this moment to revisit us, then. How very fortunate for everyone involved."

I stared. Master Caldrea said, "You see, as you might imagine, the Hunters are extremely eager to rid themselves of you. Indeed, they are quite literally born with that desire burning in their veins. I cannot tell you how gratified I am that you will be able…well, to gratify *them* in their yearning, their hunger. " He spread his hands, and his smile was gone. "It has been a long frustration, you will agree."

"And will be longer," I said, though my blood had abruptly begun roiling in my own veins. "A pity to rouse their hopes. The Hunter has not yet been born who stands any chance against me." Noise, all bluster, and I knew it. But Master Caldrea nodded again, more vigorously this time, as though he thoroughly agreed with my nonsense.

"Truer than perhaps you know, good Soukyan. We must wait together, just a little while, for that birth. In the meantime, you remain our guest, and no hurt will come to you." He paused, scratching his head in a peculiarly human gesture. "Well, no, that may not be entirely true; my apologies. All the same, I would not waste time in attempting to repeat that first flight. Knowing you, however, I suspect those are wasted words, but I must leave that to your own judgment." He bowed formally, and was gone.

There was no lock; only the guard. When I put my head out into the corridor, after a little time, he smiled almost shyly at me, but both hands dropped to his waist, at which dangled a remarkable variety of sharp objects, long and short, and a couple of serviceable bludgeons to boot. I was touched by the implicit flattery, and reasonably certain that I could silence him well before he got any one of his toys free and pointed at me. But I looked at him and saw myself at his age: so earnestly steadfast, so proud to be trusted by my masters with such a responsibility...and I could not have laid a hand on him. Besides, there were other guards beyond. I went back into my cell and closed the door.

And there I stayed, for days I grew too bored to bother counting. I invented ways to entertain myself, exercise and meditation—both in the economical South Island style—being the most obvious; but I also requested pen and paper, and tried my hand at poetry, which I love and memorize, and have absolutely no gift for. I am especially fond of the ballad form that my sister taught me, which is practiced in the west country, around Jara and Suyanashak. I wrote four during the time of my captivity in *that place,* most of them drawn from heroic legends of long ago, and all of them quite bad.

I also meditated a good deal on what Brother Laska and the dying Hunter had meant. There were trees aplenty on the grounds—*that place* was squarely in the middle of an ancient wood, after all—but no individual trunk that I had ever known to have legend or reputation attached to it. Yet Laska was very nearly as old as the forest itself—or had always seemed so—and had spoken of this Tree as a thing he could guide me to. More, he had seemed eager to do just that, and most dismayed when he saw me a captive. I hoped he might come to my cell to chat with me, but he never once did.

Master Caldrea did come, however, now and again. Often he came in company with one or another senior brother or subordinate Master: I remember in particular a thin, intense Master named Tudo who kept returning constantly to the matter of *that place's* supposed loss of power and influence, even justifying the deterioration of its environs. "We have never been easy to discover; we have always preferred to go unnoticed, to be overlooked, passed by. Yet those who seek us—like you—still find us, and we ourselves still find anyone we care to find, still learn what we choose to know. Nothing has changed, nothing at all." But Master Caldrea's sidelong glance and the slight twist of his mouth told me otherwise.

Sometimes, surprisingly, he would come to bring me some delicacy or other that he thought I might enjoy. When I commented that I was eating better as a prisoner than I ever had as a novice, as though I were being fattened like a goose for Thieves' Day, he replied that this was only to be expected. "You are important to us, Soukyan, by now you are part of our folklore. *The one who got away, the one who defied the Hunters...*I assure you, among our young ones at least, you are positively mythical." He grinned at me, half-tauntingly, half with something almost like affection. "That is why I make a point of setting them to guard you, those young ones. I have a sort of theory that it would go against your conscience to harm them. So far, it has proved correct." He patted my arm and added smugly, "Admirable."

"I would not count too much on my admirable conscience," I warned him. "I might be biding my time, debating exactly the right moment for my flight. It has happened before—any number of Hunters could tell you that. If they could still talk."

"Well, *I* would not wait too long on choosing that moment," he answered dryly. "Another moment approaches, one that concerns you greatly." And though we were both maintaining a jocular tone, I noticed the next morning that the young guards in the guest wing had been replaced by older, harder-looking monks who carried fewer weapons—some none at all, like the Hunters.

I made my first attempt to escape during full daylight, reasoning that while the guard on my cell was always strengthened at night, even doubled, a certain confident laxness prevailed during the day. I have also always believed that an air of authority is everything; thus, when a guard who had just arrived at his post saw me strolling confidently down the corridor, beaming as benignly as some visiting dignitary, he actually let me come within reach before it occurred to him to try to cry out and brace himself to repel boarders. He never got a sound out of his mouth, though I am glad I did not have to kill him. I dropped him sleeping in a corner and moved on, sauntering straight ahead, as though I had every right to be doing so. A very old trick, but it works more often than you might expect.

It got me through three guards, and very nearly as far as the big double doors before a dozen monks fell on me from all sides, putting paid to *that* particular getaway. As before, they made every effort not to damage me, but simply bore me down with the weight and mass of themselves. They returned me to my cell, outside which the first guard was sitting up, looking dazed and reproachful. I apologized as I was rushed by him, but we never really established a trustful relationship after that.

"I am pleased to see you in condition for such a gallant and stylish endeavor," Master Caldrea said,

Return

"but I did warn you that it would be useless. As every other will be."

"Whatever festivity you and your Hunters may have planned for me," I assured him, "I will not be in attendance. You will have to send a messenger to inform me of the outcome." Master Caldrea smiled without replying.

Maintaining form, I made two more straightforward efforts to escape, both of which failed resoundingly. The first involved me dressing in a guard's clothing, over the strenuous—and rather too loud—objections of the guard. The second try had to do with my discovery—thanks to the shy little kitchen boy who came every evening to clear away my food tray—of a small hatchway a few yards down the corridor, through which it was loaded onto a belt that was then wound on rollers back to the kitchen. It is still something of a sore point that I would have easily gotten away unseen if I had known to wait even half an hour for the brother on the night shift to close up the kitchen and go to bed. But he happened to be an extremely conscientious monk, who liked to see the belt completely clear of dirty dishes and utensils before he considered his work done. I crawled out of that hatch to a grinning welcome, and was

51

cursing myself—not my captors—all the way back to my cell.

Actually, it was a different cell this time: one without a mattress of any sort, nor any light, except when the door was opened. This did not happen, as a rule, more than once a day, even on the occasions when Master Caldrea brought my single meal himself. Despite the severity of my punishment, he could not resist praising my inventiveness, saying that no prisoner had ever thought of such an attempt, and that he almost wished that mine had succeeded. "Not that it would have made any difference in the long run—but all the same, I do wish you and I were to have a bit more time together. It would have been pleasant. Ah, well, the moon is the moon." With that, he bowed, as he always did on leaving me, and shut the door, returning me to darkness, along with my sudden question.

Which was not really a question, but an understanding. Having had no window in either cell, nor any way of seeing sun or moon, it had not occurred to me that he—and, obviously, the Hunters—were waiting for a certain phase of the moon. Why the waiting was necessary was a riddle I could not answer, but I did not feel I needed to. What I *did* need was to be out of this room. I sat on the cold floor that was all my furniture, and pondered whether it was yet time to make use of certain knowledge.

To this day I do not know whether my hesitation served me well or ill, as men measure things, for the third Hunter came before the moon.

He was dead. I had buried him. I had said "Sunlight on your road" to him.

Yet there he stood in my cell, holding a tallow candle in one hand, having shut the door behind him with the other. It had made a sound like an axe falling, waking me out of a half-doze. Master Caldrea and another robed figure, unfamiliar to me, stood behind the small, smiling man. I stared up into their faces and felt my life closing with the door.

"Soukyan," the Hunter said.

I have, from time to time since, seriously considered taking another name, to be rid of the sound of his voice speaking this one. His smile widened, but the blue eyes…no, there is no comparison for those eyes, no declaring that those eyes were *like* anything else. They were just what they were, and I see them still. He spoke softly, with that upward, questioning lilt they all have, always. He said, "Fool?"

I shook my head—not to deny his judgment, the gods know—but to clear it as best I could, and to focus on that face I had last seen when I was shoveling earth on it with my hands and my unstrung bow. He repeated, "Foolish Soukyan? Foolish." And his smile gobbled me up—I could truly feel myself sliding down his throat: whole, headfirst. The Hunter said, "Tricked. All the way."

"Yes," I said slowly. "Yes, I see that now. Not a mark on you beyond that forearm scratch, and *still* I took you for dead. I *knew* you were dead. No breath, no heartbeat." I shook my head again. Obviously he did not need these things in the normal fashion or degree. I said, "Fool, yes. You tricked me into coming here. From the beginning."

"From the beginning." The Hunter laughed fully then, and actually slapped his thigh. I had never seen such a thing before. He said again, "All the way. Never a moment out of Masters' sight. Not riding, not sleeping—not even when you…when the woman-face came." Hunters are strangely prudish about women: that was the best even he could manage in reference to the guise he was now telling me had made no difference. "Deceived nobody. Not Brother Laska, not Master Caldrea, nobody. Welcome home, Soukyan. Good to see Soukyan. Never leave us again, Soukyan. Never leave again."

Return

He sat down beside me, and said, softly, "All my brothers? So many, I can only kill you once? Unjust." He did seem a bit depressed as he set to his work.

We think of torture as a matter of instruments: racks, heated irons, pincers, crushers, knives, razor-edged flails. The Hunters, however, take great pride in their skill, and this one produced only a small silver knife very similar to the one with which Master Caldrea had peeled the *sulyak* pear during our dinner. It may well have been the same knife, for all I know—I recall that the tip was daintily divided for a little way along the blade, and I certainly remember for what purpose. It is not quite so efficient on flesh; after awhile he tossed it aside with an irritable grunt. I hear that sound in the middle of the most pleasant dreams, often, even now.

After that he went at me like an insane masseur, like a butcher tenderizing a tough slab of meat—no, better, say rather a fisherman working over the giant shellfish that South Island folk call *shamokin,* but coast people name *marlouk.* The belief common to both is that the creature must die in a state of relaxation, or it will become almost unchewable in minutes, no matter how long you pound it. I braced myself in every way I knew against the ceaseless, merciless storm of hand-edge hammer-blows to my gut and groin and face (blood there, a good deal of it, spoiling his record); to my neck and throat as well; to every vulnerable ligament, muscle and tendon in my body, and even to my hair, which he would grab to haul me back to pain each time I lost consciousness. Looking up into his blue eyes as he slapped my head back and forth, grabbing my jaw, my whole mouth, between his thumb and fingers, I could feel through my bones how badly he wanted to kill me, and I would grin my red grin in his face, because I knew it would not be allowed. Then he would hit me harder, because he knew it too, and I would go away again, and so it went, world without end.

But there are a few ways of dealing with even the worst agony—of *absenting* oneself from it—that *the man who laughs* taught me long ago, and I employed them to their fullest extent, as I had prepared myself to do the instant I looked into the third Hunter's mad blue eyes. For three different purposes were crowded into my cell that day, and I kept reminding myself that I needed to stay present, so I could pay attention to all of them. This is difficult when you keep being beaten to the brink of death by someone who knows how to do it, and has every intention of doing it once for each of his cohorts you have killed. I know this, because the Hunter told me so. Each time.

The Masters themselves obviously wanted something from me, some information that I must eventually yield up to them to stop the beating. And I *would* yield it to them in time, but not until I focused more clearly on exactly what they were saying to one another as they watched the Hunter taking out his fury on me. Because I wanted something too. If I had been lured back to *that place* by a false death and other possible deceptions, that did not mean that there was no greater truth to be found. If I could only hold onto consciousness long enough—the periods of coherent awareness were definitely becoming shorter—and if the Hunter could only be kept from going over the brink himself and taking me with him, what I was enduring might yet turn out to be worthwhile.

Finally he hit me hard enough that I actually skidded across the cell floor on my back, coming to rest with my head almost between one Master's foot and what I recognized as Master Caldrea's fine *sheknath*-leather sandals. I felt his voice in the stone under me, rather than hearing it. "That will be enough for now. *Enough!* When he comes to himself, I will question him."

I kept my eyes tightly closed, feeling the Hunter's breath on my face. But he did not touch me. I heard the other Master say pettishly, "I would like it to be recorded that I have found this entire affair distasteful in the extreme. If the man had anything of value to tell us, he would surely have babbled it all at least an hour ago."

"So noted," murmured Master Caldrea. "But you do not know him as I do. He is Soukyan, and he has killed more Hunters than you, Jedrath, have had your wine glass refilled. It would be more than worth our time to learn how he became our nemesis, even if we had nothing more than that to concern us. Even if the Tree were not dying."

It took more will than surviving the Hunter's best efforts not to pop my eyes open and demand details. There *was* a Tree then, and it *was* somehow intimately connected with the existence of the Hunters, the Masters, and *that place* itself. I knew that this, finally, was the reason I had been lured back here—though I could not yet see the purpose.

The Master named Jedrath asked, somewhat hesitantly, "That *is* certain, then? There is no saving the Tree?"

"There is now," Master Caldrea said.

Return

The Hunter growled, "He wakes." I gave up pretense and opened my eyes just as he reached for me. Master Caldrea made a small sound, and the Hunter confined himself to dragging me abruptly into a more or less seated position. The cell spun in and out for a few moments, and I would have vomited, but I had already done that two or three times. The Masters quite kindly waited for me to find my equilibrium before questioning me. Master Jedrath even tossed me a rag to wipe away the blood from my nose and mouth.

I spoke first, thinking to take them all perhaps a little off-balance. I said thickly, "I presume you have questions for me. Ask them, and I will answer if I can." I peered at them through fast-closing eyes. "Or was all this activity merely for my amusement?"

Master Caldrea said, "Hardly that. We have been speculating for years—almost since you left us, really—on just how you acquired the skills that let you evade and kill our Hunters, time on time." He shrugged, slowly and gracefully. "We felt it necessary to inquire directly."

I suddenly felt very tired, and not entirely from the Hunter's work. I said, "No. *That* makes no sense at all. All this effort to bring me here, tricking me into believing that it was my own will...all for some absurd course in combat strategy? Even with my mind still bouncing between the walls of my skull, I would know better than to believe a single breath of that. Please, ask what questions you will, but make them real ones. I should like to take a nap before dinner." The blood from my nose had stopped flowing, but I knew it was broken. It has happened before, and since.

Jedrath whispered loudly to Master Caldrea, "Ask him what he knows of the Tree."

Master Caldrea gave him a cold, disgusted look. Possessed on the instant of a small and ridiculous demon, I croaked, "The Tree, yes...I have come to destroy the Tree. I will cut it down and tear up the roots, so no one will ever know where it grew." I said that last part two or three times, because I liked the way it sounded. I don't think I was yet quite back in my right mind.

"He knows nothing," Master Caldrea said. Exactly as courteously as though he were bowing himself out of *my* rooms after another pleasant dinner, he said, "I'm sure we will be speaking again in the near future."

"I look forward to it," I said. I believe I even bowed where I sat, as much as my ribs would let me.

The Hunter stayed briefly after they had gone. He put his face so close to mine that I could smell the

Return

odd faint oiliness of his laughter, warm in my ear. He whispered—no question-cadence in his voice now—"Nothing you do harm the Tree, never. No axe you swing ever touch the Tree, no spade of you ever dig into, no poison you put to the Tree ever bite—no fire, no fire you set…"

And he stopped. Just for a moment, no more, before patting my cheek, almost caressing it with a certain awful tenderness. He stood up and said, "We wait for you at the Tree soon," and I looked again into those blue eyes, and I nodded. With that he left, and I crawled into one corner of the cell, where I ambled in and out of sentience for the next several hours.

I was left alone for the next several days, during which I mainly slept. I ate so little, in fact, that Master Caldrea clearly came to fear that I might be a little too damaged to recover, or had spitefully determined to fast, to starve myself to death. I had no such plan, but I did enjoy watching him worry—he was an anxious man, under the coolly knowledgeable exterior—and I especially savored his one diffident apology. "I assure you, I took no pleasure in what was being done. It was not something I would have chosen to do, of my own will. But the Hunters…the Hunters are born obsessed with you, and had I forbidden it...." A single graceful shrug, a quick gesture of both open hands, and that was the end of it.

Still, he came every day, until he was satisfied that I was fully recovered from my ordeal. And he brought me plain new garments, to replace the bloodied, soiled tatters I was wearing. I hesitate to say that he felt any least guilt or shame—such emotions are completely foreign in *that place*—but I suppose it could have been so. I will never know now. What I did know, lying there, was pitifully little: that there was indeed a Tree, that it was irremediably close to death before I came, and that my blue-eyed torturer fully expected to meet me again there soon. As for what purpose, I felt reasonably certain that it could not be something enjoyable. Not for me, anyway.

"The moon is the moon." I came back to that more often than I revisited anything else that Master Caldrea had told me. In my experience—and even then, I had more of it than I liked—anything involving the moon usually takes place at its fullest, or when it stands at zero, vanished altogether for two or three days. Immured in this windowless cell, I had no way of knowing the phases of the moon, or day from night. But when I felt strong enough I knew in all my

battered bones that it was time for me to go. Now. That moment. Literally.

And I knew a way to do it, a way that I had always known. A way that I had never wanted to take, and never had, and did not want to take now. But there was no choice.

The man who laughs taught it to me. Separately he had taken both of us in, Lal and me, many years before we finally met, and he taught us each exactly what we needed to know, even though neither of us could have imagined it at the time. In Lal's case he gave her an emerald ring to ease the nightmares born of a slave's childhood, and a little gardener's charm as well, one that would raise the dead as easily as a cabbage. He also introduced her to the deep sea, which claimed her heart the moment she set foot on a battered, pitching old fishing boat. She will die there, at sea, like enough, though not while I can prevent it. Even as much as I hate boats.

For myself, he gave me the woman-shape, which made absolutely no sense to me at the time, but which had more than once preserved the strange life *he* knew was marked out for me. There was another gift too—one that came at a cost. They all do, really, but most often you don't know it until the gift has been

employed and the price is at your door. With this one I knew the price well in advance.

At first I was not even sure I recalled its workings. I did know that it involved certain incantations and certain...other spells, if you will, which would have been difficult to conceal in the limited privacy of my previous cell. Here, alone in the dark, I managed surprisingly well, saying the right words at the right moment and feeling my way through the few other things you have to do, just as *the man who laughs* had shown me, over and over, so very long ago. I was quite proud of myself, and liked to think that he would have been, too.

But how do you tell, in utter darkness, whether or not you have become invisible?

You go on bumping into things, of course, and you can't see your hand before your face any more than you ever could. I had no idea whether or not the charm had succeeded until I stepped out of my unlocked door and approached the guard, who was still yawning in my face and scratching his belly when I laid him gently down to sleep. It is quite a tidy and efficient spell, really.

It also endures no more then a quarter of an hour; seventeen minutes at the outside. Seventeen minutes, paid for with at least three years off your life span, or as many, possibly, as five. But years there will be, and I could only hope that I was sacrificing time during which I'd just as soon have been dead anyway. *The man who laughs* told me that he himself had used it more than once; but then, of course, he was a wizard. Wizards live a very long time.

The moon was only a pale gray fingernail above me as I limped through the great doors. It seemed to be flickering feebly, like a candle about to fail. There was no turmoil, no noise of discovery and pursuit; none of my poor guards must have wakened yet. But they would, so I made off toward the marshes, exactly as I had done before, determined to be well away before the spell wore off or any alarm was raised. Being no longer the young man who plunged blindly and wildly down a weed-slick slope—cracking his head open on a rock, almost ending his flight right there—I circled cautiously, watching where I put my feet, and went to ground no more than half a mile from *that place*. By then I was solidly visible again. Finding dry leaves under a shroud of damp ones, as the fox had taught me, I put moons and Hunters out of my mind, and caught what sleep I could.

Return

If they had had dogs...but of course they never did, completely reliant on the Hunters as they were. I woke to voices carried on the wind, too distant to be intelligible, and with no indication that they were drawing closer. I washed and drank at the nearest stream, numbed my hunger with *tilgit,* which grows wild throughout the marshes; and examined the sky, satisfying myself that the following night would show no moon at all. That would be my night. The Hunters might or might not be waiting for me, but I was coming for the Hunters. And the Tree.

Madness? Bravado? Both, and neither...and all that I had become since that first Hunter made a professional killer out of me. Yes, it was a killing that sent me flying to the shelter of *that place* as a child, the murder of the man who had so injured my sister—but it was killing the Hunter, seeing those contemptuous eyes widening with the shocked understanding that his pitiful, helpless victim, armed with nothing but the broken haft of a paring knife, had struck him down, had ended him, that truly changed me...it is not a good thing to feel that powerful. It is *not*. I would unlearn it, if I could.

Between now and tomorrow's absent moon, I had plans to make and a day to use wisely. The morning was annoyingly bright and clear, but I moved with the sun, taking advantage of every shadow and every fragment of shade as I eased closer to *that place*. I could make out figures and faces coming and going; compared to its normal somnolent air, the mansion was humming like a nest of those little black *miriki* bees that do not die when they sting you. I recognized two or three guards, and even the boy who had told me how dishes were returned to the kitchen. But I saw no sign of Master Caldrea, which concerned me a good deal.

Indeed, it concerned me enough that I risked recapture more than once, hoping even to spy him through a window. I knew better than to assume that he had given up on my recapture, nor to imagine that *he* imagined that I could choose escape over revenge. I slipped back into cool shadow on my belly, and thought hard about Hunters.

Once you have observed Hunters at close range—and presumably survived the encounter—you can never mistake them again. But I had spied none since my arrival, except for the one who had tortured me, and surely they would have been alerted since my escape. As a boy, I had seen them on rare occasions: small to medium in height, lithely built, with light eyes, pale brown skin, and distinctively quick, agile movements. They had nothing I could ever discover to do with the actual workings of *that place:* we youngest servants generally thought they were a special kind of monk, while the older boys hinted darkly at their real function, and dared us to approach and speak to one. I certainly never did, and I never knew anyone who took up the challenge. The Hunters look like what they are.

But I had seen none during the time I was held captive in the guest wing—nor during any of my escape attempts, either, when one might think Hunters would have been much in evidence. I spent much of that last day roaming the entire area, always returning to *that place,* chancy as it was, wondering where they were and still hoping for a sight of Master Caldrea.

I finally got my wish late in the afternoon, when he came briskly through the double door, walked into the open, then halted midway to the bushes and to shout this speech to the air. "My dear Soukyan, if you are within the sound of my voice, as I would think you are, may I first heartily praise your determination and your ingenuity—and may I also assure you that these admirable qualities will make no least difference to the outcome of this night. Savor your remaining hours here, since I do not for a moment imagine you will be wise enough to employ them in running for your life. Which would not help, either; if I wished to call them off now, they would pay no slightest heed to me. Take it as a compliment, Soukyan, and do enjoy this beautiful evening. The night will be less so."

He bowed formally, as he had done so often upon leaving my cell, and went back into the mansion. I lay still for some time.

I did take advantage of the twilight's sweet-smelling warmth by slipping back into the woods to tend to dinner. Without my bow or the *trimoira* dagger, I was not only defenseless, but faced nourishing myself on *tilgit* for what might well be my last meal. That thought being completely intolerable, I fashioned a snare from a V-shaped branch and a few supple twigs, caught a plump *starik*, and devoured it raw.

Death had been much on my mind all that day, in the most practical sense. Giving Master Caldrea proper credit for intelligence, and for having known me in my childhood, I assumed that he would expect me to attempt to recover my weapons, and would have them all under heavy guard, inaccessible, as I would have done in his place. But I could not even find out where they were being kept, no matter whom

Return

I followed, no matter how many risks I took to spy on hurrying monks and tantalizing clumps of sentries. Barring a stout tree-limb trimmed into some sort of bludgeon, I was shortly about to face empty-handed an unknown number of the most gifted and pitiless killers I had ever encountered. Utterly absurd frustration at one end of the day, suicide at the other: Soukyan to the life, Lal would have said.

At one point I even crawled as close as I dared to the stable, thinking that the weapons might have been hidden in the hayloft, but heard only my own mare, who nickered when she sensed me near. Any guards who knew horses, Hunters or no, would have been out and swarming on the instant, so I discounted the stable and moved on.

Somewhere around that time, with dark coming on, I realized that I was beginning to look seriously at promising branches.

Dusk is a bad time for me—always, since I was very young, long before I became whatever exactly I am. I have never known why that should be, and it still irritates me. A mercenary may grow wistful, even sentimental, regretting losses and mistakes, stupidities and misjudgments and crimes that cannot easily be remembered as mistakes…but what kind of regrets can a small boy possibly have who begins to cry as the sky turns slowly violet and the first twinge of cold comes into the air? I have no more fear of midnight than Lal-after-dark does, and the deep hours before dawn have often been my own high noon. But twilight can be hard, and right then I was desperate enough to determine on a completely insane gamble in order to acquire at least *some* weapon. I focused on one guard, younger than the others, who seemed not to be guarding anything in particular, but rather strutting here and there, striking poses with his long broadsword. As he wandered increasingly close to the shadow where I lay, I prepared to pounce, catch him by the neck, strangle him silent, and drag him into the woods to finish him. I am good at this. If I were not, I would have been long dead myself.

But with that boast on record, let me report further that as I crouched, behind me a wheezing old voice rasped quietly, "Stir an inch and die, traitor Soukyan!"

Brother Laska.

I turned my head and saw him there, twenty feet behind me, grinning his splintery brown grin and holding my bow by the end, like a spear. I had heard nothing of the old gatekeeper's approach; as my nerves

Return

were astretch to their greatest possible extent, this
implied more skill on his part than I knew. Nevertheless
he did nothing when I took the bow away from him,
but only muttered, "I have the arrows. Come for them
two hours after sunset, when the Masters have gone."
He turned away, standing straighter and walking more
firmly than I ever remembered seeing him. Over his
shoulder, he added, "Then I will take you to the Tree."

And so I hid once more, and waited. Brother Laska
did not lie: after sunset the Masters did leave, one by
one, through the great doors, apparently in order of
rank, for Master Caldrea was the last.

When it was true moonless dark, dark enough for
me to hope I might be taken for a guard if I were
seen—though none of those carried bows—I stole
toward the great door, meeting no one on the way,
and slipped inside for what I knew would be the last
time. Brother Laska was waiting for me at the closet
under the stair, my dagger, my pack, my arrows and
the quiver in his trembling hands. I took them with
gratitude—he even had my flint and steel as well—
asking, "Have they been here all the time? Since
Master Caldrea took them?"

Brother Laska shook his yellow-white head, grinning again. "He hid them, but I found them. I find

everything." He watched as I tested and adjusted the new string and sighted along several arrows, to make sure that no dampness had warped them. He said, "I knew you would come for them."

"My weapons?"

"The Hunters." I heard footsteps and ducked into the closet, shielding my face, as a pair of apprentices passed, teasing Brother Laska and chattering about the shapeshifter who could be a man or a woman, and make himself disappear altogether, when he chose. Brother Laska growled them along, and I asked him bluntly, "Why are you helping me? What game are *you* playing?"

"Don't like Hunters. Never did, never did. Shouldn't *be* here!" Brother Laska had suddenly gotten violently aroused, the way very old people sometimes do. "Master Krelim's fault—Master Krelim, before you, you wouldn't know. Woke up the Tree. Shouldn't have."

I turned and stared at him. Some grow transparent with age, but Brother Laska had become perfectly opaque since my childhood—you could see nothing of him beyond the liver-spotted skin and scalp and the sunken, faded yellow eyes. Brother Laska said, "The Hunters' Tree. I will take you."

Return

He calmed down as quickly as he had caught fire, and would have turned from me, but I put my hands on his shoulders and held him there, as gently as I could. I said "Tell me about the Tree, Brother Laska. Please."

Brother Laska fussed and fidgeted under my hands at first, but then he grew quiet and curiously thoughtful: here and not-here; present, but not entirely accounted for. He studied me for some moments before he spoke again. "Power. *Power.* Who says no to having power, great power? Invincible assassins when you need? Master Caldrea wants somebody dead, the Tree drops three Hunters right into his lap—finished, they go right back in—"

"They go *back?*"

Another nod, so fierce that I actually heard his neck creak. "Tree *draws* them in. With target dead, Tree draws the Hunters back inside itself, gets nourished both ways. Everybody *feeds*—Tree, Masters, everybody, right?" He gave me one of his terrifying grins. "Well, so, maybe not target, not exactly, but target has his part to play too. Because each death, each killing, *something* goes into the Tree, something the Tree needs—*I* don't know what to call it." He peered elaborately sideways at me, like a boy serving as lookout while his companions raid a fruit stand. "You understand me? You can hear?"

"I think so," I answered him. "The Tree draws power from every death, taking it back through the Hunters. And the Masters plan to...feed me to the Tree?"

No nod this time, but the clear, level stare of a much younger man. "*Have* to. Because the Tree serves one task at a time—only one, only one killing at a time. And you survive and survive and survive like nobody else, never. So the Tree goes hungry, hungry. The Tree dies." He grinned at me again, like a badly-healed wound slowly reopening. "Your doing. You live, the Tree fails. Live much longer, kill too many more of its Hunters, the Tree dies."

And more than that I could not get out of him, except for occasional bursts of anger at the very existence of this Tree. He kept blaming Master Krelim, gone decades before my time at *that place*, but greatly revered in my youth, almost as a saint. "The bow is not enough," he told me. "They will come at you too fast, you must have a sword." He offered me his own: a classic Corcorua two-hander, a true prize, which he seemed barely able to lift himself. I declined, checking to make certain that my *trimoira* dagger was still properly sharp and well-balanced, while hoping earnestly that I would never need to throw it.

When Brother Laska finally said, "We will go now," I hooked the bow across my left shoulder. It felt good there, like a friend's arm around me.

"From this time we say nothing," Brother Laska said when we emerged into the darkness. "Follow me closely—must not lose each other. It is very hard to find, that Tree, you must stay close to me." Indeed, I could barely see him. He put his hand on my arm and confided, in a whistling whisper, "I got lost, you know, that first time I went alone looking for that Tree. I never found my way back." He winked, which was a strangely frightening sight: that one eye slowly closing by itself in that melting candle of a face, and then suddenly popping open again, like some kind of quick little animal or insect. He said again, "Do not lose me."

I expected that he would lead me in the general direction of the marshes; but in fact we went the opposite way, crossing the path toward the stable, but then veering sharply to the left and working uphill into country I had never really known when I lived in *that place*. The hills were rustly-dry in all seasons, pocked with dangerous holes and ruts in which one might easily break an ankle—especially on a moonless night—and there were always rumors among the apprentices that *lourijakhs* prowled there by night; though what they would have found to live on, I cannot imagine. There may have been some scratch of a path, but I never saw it, not in this darkness, and not under the drifts of *sima* leaves, so long dead as to be colorless and make no sound underfoot. I held onto Brother Laska's shoulder, somewhat gingerly, because he had brought the great Corcorua sword with him, slinging it down his back, scabbardless. If he tipped over backward—which he very well might, on this ground—that monster would be bound to slice one or the other of us.

I heard birds: *tarshis,* the only nightbird you will find this far southeast. They make a high, grunting sound, like a sleeper turning in bed, not loud, but persistent. Once they start they'll keep it up all night, just at the edge of your ear. I still thought I was hearing them when Brother Laska suddenly stopped and hissed, "*Listen!*" The Corcorua sword banged my nose.

It took a moment, but I heard them.

Voices. I could not say how many—several, certainly, but it was a murmur, not the rumble of a large crowd. And there was firelight; and one song rising out of the murmur and above it, high and clear and quite distinct, though the words were in no language I knew. But I recognized immediately the voice of Master Caldrea.

He was as much chanting as singing: a curiously angular, slippery melody that kept sliding sideways, changing pitch each time; almost repetitious but never entirely so. After a time it began to hurt my ears and hurt my mind as well, though I know there's no explaining that. Beside me, Brother Laska muttered, "There, *there,* do you see what they do? Do you see them now?"

"I hear them," I said, "but I see nothing. I need to get closer."

"He calls to it. Calls the Tree." Brother Laska's voice was flat and low. I crawled forward, using my elbows and my feet to push the rest of me along, until I got a good look at the scene taking place a mere hundred feet or so ahead—and at the Tree. It stood alone in a clearing: not as tall as I had vaguely imagined it, but seeming as massive as a cathedral, its many broad, low branches decked prominently with long, wicked black thorns. Its bark and leaves were of the same deep, deep red; but its roots, bulking up out of the ground like a countryman's great swollen knuckles, were as black as those thorns, and looked somehow as dangerous. A group of monks—no more than eight or ten—stood in a ring around the Tree, but the only one speaking now—still chanting, rather—was Master Caldrea. He stood a little way back from the others, beside a small fire whose flames made his face seem constantly to leap out of the darkness and then recede, like the retreat of a wave.

Brother Laska nodded jerkily, like a puppet, pointing ahead. "The branches. See the branches!"

You have seen how, in the spring, caterpillars will eat their way through thousands of leaves, until one morning there is no caterpillar—only a chrysalis or a cocoon dangling from a twig, a flower stalk, a wall? So it was with that strange and terrible tree: I counted nine such chrysalides—all an unpleasant greenish-yellow, all man-sized, each suspended from a black thorn, and each beginning to ripple and shudder as I stared, as something inside each one fought to break free. Their struggles grew more intense as Master Caldrea's chanting heightened and rose in pitch. One chrysalis was just starting to split at the top.

Beside me, Brother Laska moaned, "Master Krelim...I was small, I followed him everywhere." I remembered once hearing that Brother Laska had been brought to *that place* as an infant, though I never learned any more detail than that. His voice was like a hot, wet wind in my ear. "I followed him—I was there when he found the Tree. He knew magic, old magic from old times, he knew how to wake deep, old, angry things. He sang, he woke up the Tree, he said to it, *we have enemies, we need protection, you must create defenders for us.* So the Tree makes the Hunters—it bears them like fruit, do you understand? Apples…plums…pomegranates…Hunters, so. Do you understand?"

I nodded, unable to take my eyes from that one chrysalis, opening so slowly. Beside me, Brother Laska mumbled, "Nine for you, what an honor! Nine Hunters called for only one man."

"Eight," I said. The chrysalis had cracked almost halfway down the side. I saw a hand emerge, and then a face, still shadowed by the branch just above it. I fitted an arrow to my bow, whispered what I do at such times, and fired. The shaft sank to the feathers just below the opening, and a body tumbled through, splitting the chrysalis the rest of the way. The Hunter fell directly at Master Caldrea's feet, dead before he was born, and the singing stopped.

I had three more arrows in the air as the monks turned and saw me and Brother Laska—who

promptly ducked down into a hollow. They uttered a massed cry of rage and sorrow and started to rush toward us, but Master Caldrea shouted. *"No! Back, and leave him to me!"*

He whirled to face the Tree, chanted several phrases that would have broken my throat to repeat. Every one of the remaining chrysalides cracked wide open at once. Five Hunters leaped to the ground, all landing as lightly as cats, but three remained within their fleshy wombs, already dead or dying, pierced through by my arrows. One of the Hunters, apparently the destined partner of the first I had killed, bent briefly over the body. He looked up at me with his mouth open in a silent scream, and raced in my direction. I aimed for the heart; but the dim light and his speed threw off my aim. My arrow took him in the throat instead, and he died choking on his own blood.

Then they were on me, all the rest of them. I dropped the bow and shrugged free of the quiver, but never had a chance to get the *trimoira* out, nor did they even bother to snatch it from my belt. I fully expected to die on the spot at their hands; but Master Caldrea roared orders, and, like the monks in the stable, they pressed close around me, glaring and grinning, their light eyes brilliant with such hatred as I've never seen again, nor ever expect to see. Seizing me by shoulders, hair, and arms, they brought me to Master Caldrea where he stood by the Tree, and he smiled at me with the bright clarity of madness. He said, "Welcome, Soukyan. Welcome to your great destiny."

"I would have been here much later," I answered him, "if I had recognized your invitation. My most sincere apologies."

Master Caldrea actually laughed outright, though no one else in the clearing did. "Yes, yes, more than accepted. You are without a doubt the most important person here tonight—the Tree is happy to see you." He swung out an arm, gesturing toward the Tree, as though he were introducing us. "He is come," he said to the Tree, crooning, confiding. "I said he would come. The wait is ended."

Standing this close to it, surrounded by Hunters, their hands on me, I noticed—as I could not have done from a distance—that, for all its apparent burly vastness, there was also a strange air of instability about the Tree, hard to depict even now. The night breeze stirred its branches more easily than it should have; paradoxically, the dark-red leaves drooped wearily, hardly responding at all; and only

Return

the great knuckly roots seemed truly alive, thrusting up defiantly to support and shelter the oddly fragile-seeming trunk. Further, for all the speed with which they had overcome me, and for all the strength of their hands on me, these Hunters also felt somehow not *right*, any more than seeing four of them at once felt right. I could not have said what alerted me to the difference; but I knew that Master Caldrea knew it too. I could see that knowledge in his bright, bright eyes.

"You have hurt the Tree," he said, not accusingly, but in a casual, conversational manner. "The more Hunters you killed, the more the Tree had to produce—it is like asking a wheatfield for two and three crops a year, a sheep to be ready for shearing every week or two. Even our House is not what it was, as you have noticed, for we bled as best we could, trying to sustain it against privation. This is your doing, Soukyan, year on year." He gripped my wrists and squeezed hard, still smiling, just as though he were welcoming me to his home.

"You do me too much honor," I replied. "I have only done what I could. And I am not finished yet." I was sure I was going to die, and young enough yet to wish to leave on some note of bravado. Silliness.

Master Caldrea smiled affectionately. "No, indeed, you are far from finished yet. I envy you." Without turning, he beckoned, and from the circle of monks on the far side of the Tree, the third Hunter came to stand beside me like some kind of shadow brother. He even leaned on my shoulder, gripped the back of my neck lightly, and whispered in my ear, "Soon…soon. All well now."

Then the grip tightened, tightened *hard*, and Master Caldrea strode forward and tore my shirt open to the navel. He had a small silver knife in his hand.

No divided tip here: this one came to a single point, with a channel on both sides of the blade, to lead the blood away. Master Caldrea employed it as an artist does his brush—or a seamstress her needle, for the matter of that. It was fine, delicate work, centered over my heart, and it took a long time. None of the cuts were at all deep—you would not be able to see them today, save that the third Hunter then poured a thin gray-green liquid, which vanished as it touched the skin over my chest. As the Hunter did this, Master Caldrea began to sing, but not as he had done before. The melody was as simple as a child's counting rhyme, and as adhesive. I could sing it for you today, but I have never met anyone who could recite the words, or tell me what they meant.

Return

But a very strange thing happened to me with that song. Master Caldrea repeated it several times, and as each line left his lips, something left *me,* for all the world like a bird flying out of my body—perhaps through the little wounds left by the silver knife—and vanishing into the wind. And this, for whatever reason, pained me far worse than the cutting itself had done. I think I cried out, as I had not done even when the Hunter was beating me. I know I cried out.

"Hush, my friend," Master Caldrea said gently, each time I gasped or whimpered with loss. "Hush, it is no more than giving back what never belonged to you—the energy, the spirit, the little part of every Hunter you ever murdered. There...*there*...now it is free of you, all of it, all you took—can you catch even a glimpse, before it rejoins the Tree, where it belongs? This beloved Tree, that you have injured so cruelly?" The Hunters around me made a low sound that I would not like to hear again, and crowded closer, if that was possible. Master Caldrea waved them back, but they paid him no head.

"But the Tree forgives," he continued, spreading his arms, as though to embrace me. "The Tree welcomes you." Abruptly he plucked the *trimoira* from my belt with one hand, smeared a streak of blood from my chest on the other, and turned to the third Hunter, who knelt and bowed his head. Master Caldrea marked his forehead and cheekbones with my blood, and murmured five or six words that I could not catch. Then he stepped back, and the Hunter rose.

"It ends here." Master Caldrea's voice was perfectly cool and sane. "Not for him—not just yet, for he can only sacrifice himself after your blood has soaked into the roots of the Tree, and your soul has already gone to nourish it. Then *he* will die, on this same dagger, to seal the bargain—do you begin to see, Soukyan? Do you see?" I made no response, and the Hunter waited, his face striped gold and blue-black in the firelight..

"And the Tree will die too," Master Caldrea said. "Die, and be reborn, mightier than ever, with his blood to guard it, and your soul, your *self,* prisoned within it. What Hunters will be born of this new Tree? What power and influence will return to our House through them? You will know it better than anyone, Soukyan, and I meant it when I said I envied you. Fare well on your far journey."

I struggled, but of course it did no good; there were too many of them, dragging me further toward the Tree, whose roots appeared to rear themselves higher in eagerness to receive my blood. Master

Return

Caldrea stepped back and raised the dagger, while the third Hunter moved to my side and gripped my hair, hauling my head back to expose my neck for Caldrea's blow...

...and then froze, as a scream like a rock-*targ* raped by a lightning stroke tore the night air, and Master Caldrea, along with every Hunter, every monk—everyone but me, my head being held so tightly—turned to see Brother Laska bearing down on us, brandishing his antique sword that I had never imagined he could swing, even with both hands. He was almost upon the Hunters by the time I finally pulled free, and his face was a mask of insane fury. I had to duck myself as the wind of the blade rumpled my hair. Even the Hunters did not move immediately to close with him, they, like everyone else, scattered in all directions to be out of range of that Corcorua two-hander.

Brother Laska was still shrieking his challenge as I caught up the *trimoira* dagger from where Master Caldrea had dropped it. I ran past him, looking desperately for my bow. I came on it blindly, fumbling in the cold, dry grass, and the quiver just beyond, and turned to face four Hunters, spreading out now to come at me from different directions. Depending on range, and a few other things, I can often have a second and third arrow in the air before the first has found its mark; but the distance was too short and my assailants far too adept to let themselves become easy targets, popinjays, for my convenience. I did bring down one—a lucky shot, he nearly charged right into the arrow—and then the rest were too close for arrows, so I threw the bow away, as far as I could, to keep it from tripping me up.

I can give only a few details of what followed. The Hunters' hands kill by breaking your neck, crushing your windpipe, rupturing your liver with one open-palmed, stiff-fingered jab. You must keep them at some distance to have any hope at all of survival, and the *trimoira* gave me a life-saving length of arm. It was all in and out, dodging and lunging, sideways leaps and rolls and back somersaults. I was not nearly as swift as they were, but I had a knowledge of their favored tactics that they did not have of mine, for all they'd been inculcated in their caterpillar wombs with the supreme need to kill me. And even so...

Even so, I should be dead. My one providence lay in the fact that these were not quite the Hunters I had feared and fled and fought since I was too young to understand what they were. Dangerous still—deadly, deadly dangerous—but changed by a shadow's depth from almost invincible to almost vulnerable. The Tree's growing exhaustion had made that much difference.

The *trimoira* and the confusion accounted for one, surprisingly quickly; the survivors drew off, consulting together without speaking, as Hunters do. From the smoothly coordinated way they moved, I thought this pair might have been born a unit, and that much more dangerous for it. I seized the moment to scramble after my bow and quiver, and to loose off two arrows. Both struck home with a satisfying certainty—try that with a dagger, Lal—leaving me in command of a field grotesquely strewn with nearly-identical bodies. Bow taut, my last arrow notched and ready, I looked for the third Hunter, the one wearing my blood, but did not see him among the upright or the slain.

The monks were rapidly vanishing themselves; only Master Caldrea remained, standing before the Tree with his arms stretched wide, unafraid, but plainly sensing what I had in mind. "There will be others," he called defiantly as I approached. "There will always be others."

"Not from this tree," I said. I took my flint and steel from my pouch and knelt in the grass.

Then I remembered. I remembered the helplessness—the laughing blue eyes—the whisper, so unbearably close. *Nothing you do ever harm the Tree, never...no axe you swing...no spade...no poison...no fire you set...*

No fire you *set...*

So be it: let this among his prophecies come true. I put my flint away, and picked up a brand from the monks' own dying fire. I said, "Come away, Master."

"No," he said. His face was like slate, like old ice. "No, you cannot do this. I will not let you."

"Come away," I said again. He turned his back on me then and clung to the Tree, crying out in the language of his chant, as though appealing to it for protection, but the Tree had nothing to give him. I pulled him away by main force, and when he struggled free to run back, I hit him. Not hard, just hard enough that he sat down, dazed, which was all I wanted.

The scrubby grass was so parched that it went up with one touch of the brand. A hot wind played across my face, and for a few moments it was difficult to breathe.

Master Caldrea screamed. I turned to lay hold of him again, but he was on his feet, stumbling toward the Tree. I sprang after him, at the same time glimpsing movement in the corner of my left eye. I started to turn my head, and something came down on the back of my skull, just above the neck, so powerfully that I know I lost consciousness for a few seconds. The only reason I lost nothing more than that, I think, is that I was moving when I was struck.

When sense returned I found the third Hunter sitting on my chest, his knees pinning both of my arms. Behind him, the trunk of the Tree was already encased in rippling fire…along with something darker than the flames that could only have been Master Caldrea, leaning pitifully against it. The Hunter smiled down at me, just as he had done when he first put his hands on me. "All my brothers?" he said again. He raised his hand, canting it at an angle, slowly, just so.

Then he turned too late, starting to spring up just as his head vanished, and his body toppled sideways, and I was rolling aside myself, trying unsuccessfully to avoid the terrible cascade of blood that pulsed from the severed neck. Corcorua steel never loses its edge.

Brother Laska was petting the huge sword, mopping away the blood with a tuft of grass. I thanked him—hardly hearing my own words for the ringing in my head—and he grinned his brown grin at me. "I did well? Hard to remember."

"You saved my life," I said. I looked toward the Hunters' Tree, now completely enveloped in flame. Branches were exploding, bark was peeling away in great sheets and ribbons of fire, the black thorns blazing up and falling to ash just as quickly. I could not see Master Caldrea anymore. I said softly, so as not to disturb my head, "It is over."

Brother Laska nodded happily. "No Tree, no more Hunters. The House will grow strong again." He pointed warningly at me. "Best be gone, you. The brothers will talk."

There is a battlefield prayer to be spoken when there is no way, or no time, to bury the slain properly. I said it, and Brother Laska and I started back the way we had come. I turned once for a last look at the Hunters' Tree, which appeared to be burning even more fiercely than before. Then we went on.

As fatigued as I was, and as painfully as my head throbbed—the Hunter had missed breaking my neck by little more than an inch—the way back to *that place* seemed shorter, though the night was no less dark. I had not expected Brother Laska to accompany me as far as the stable, but he insisted on it, as though reluctant for his one adventure to end. "We were together!" he kept saying proudly. "Soukyan and Laska— I saved you, you saved the House. Soukyan and Laska!" He was carrying the two-handed sword now, shouldering it like a spear or a pike, and from time to time reaching to pet it affectionately. I found this touching, and was afraid that he might lose a finger.

At the stable I bid farewell to Brother Laska, saying, "You have done more than save my life; by heroically aiding me to rid the land of these ancient assassins, you have saved the lives of others whom you will never know. You have their thanks, as surely as you have mine."

I bowed to him, turning my back, and knelt to examine my mare's off hind foot. And perhaps it was a sound, perhaps a shadow, perhaps the familiar whistle of an old man's inhalation—one of those, or all, or something else, set me dropping and rolling and scrambling to the side as the Corcorua sword sliced into a truss of hay just above my head.

It took Brother Laska an extra moment to free the great sword, giving me time to get to my feet and put some distance—and a full bale of hay—between us. I was as dumbfounded and speechless as he must have known I would be; not least because his eyes were as bright now as a young man's eyes, and he was stalking me with a young man's lithe quickness. Even his voice was changed, turning clearer and stronger, as he said, "But how much more heroic will I be when I bring back the head of the monster, the defiler, who destroyed forever the very heart of our House, the great defenders for whom Master Caldrea unhesitatingly gave his life. How can I pass by such an opportunity, tell me that?"

The horses were all stamping and whinnying anxiously now, as Brother Laska kept coming after me and I kept backing, sidestepping and dancing away. But a stable is a limited arena for a man trying not to be cornered, and the advantage is all with the attacker. I said, "You saved my life. I do not want to kill you. I don't want to fight you at all."

Brother Laska replied with a swing of the Corcorua sword that came so close I had to leap up on a haybale to keep from losing a leg on the spot. I pointed out desperately that the monks who had seen us together that night would indeed talk—"and how will you explain that you stood with me against the Hunters? That you took a Hunter's head yourself before ever you took mine? Had you thought at all about that, old man?"

I had hoped to anger him, calling him that, and perhaps to goad him into a foolish mistake. But he

Return

kept coming, "Old man, aye—and what can a frail old man do in the hands of a maniacal killer? You dragged me along on your mission of massacre, and I was so shaken and so terrified that when I tried to kill you I slew a Hunter instead, by awful accident. But when it is known that I avenged them all, and avenged our blessed Master Caldrea as well…why, I would not be surprised if they named me his successor." He beamed at me, his jagged smile no longer grotesquely endearing, but the bared fangs of a predator. "Would you be surprised?"

"No," I said. "I must admit I would not be at all surprised." And with that I threw the last strength remaining to me into a twisting leap from an over-turned barrel to the top of a stall door, which I rode swinging straight into Brother Laska, knocking him down and jarring the sword from his hands. I was on it—and then him—in an instant, pressing the flat of the blade to his throat with the palm of one hand, grinning with my teeth clenched tightly, and rasping, "But not tonight, Brother, not tonight. This night, this head stays on these shoulders." And I patted his wrinkled cheek insultingly, as one pats a child. As the Hunter had done to me.

And my own *trimoira* dagger came up from the stable floor in his free left hand, missing my neck, gouging the flesh over my collarbone. There was that much fight in him still; and more yet, as we wrestled for the dagger. Even then, truly, I was not trying to kill him, but only to hold him off while keeping the *trimoira* out of his reach. But my left hand was on the sword against his throat, and I felt something go, collapsing under the increased pressure. He coughed, and his eyes widened, and he looked for a moment as puzzled as a child. Then he shivered once, just the one long shiver, and died beneath me. It was that fast, and that quiet.

There were spades in the stable. I carried him outside and buried him and his ancient sword under a wild *bilibro* bush, which bears great purple flowers in the spring. The blood from my gashed shoulder fell on the petals. When I was done, I said aloud, "You were not always a doorkeeper, Brother. Sunlight on your road."

When I turned toward the stable again, I saw the monks. Four or five of them, all faces I recognized from the firelit circle around Master Caldrea and the Tree. "I have done what I came to do," I said. "I wish no harm to any of you. Let me pass."

None of them moved, neither to permit nor to hinder me.

Return

I took a pace toward them, a very weary hand on the hilt of the *trimoira* dagger, seriously doubting whether I had strength enough remaining to pull it from my belt. But the oldest monk—Brother Thymanos by name, a tall man with thin blue lips—stepped forward to say, "We have come to offer you all that your passage has left us." I stared at him. Thymanos continued, "Caldrea is dead. The Hunters are ended with the Tree. If this house is to survive, it must do so, not only under a new Master, but under a new *sort* of Master." He dropped to his knees beside me, then took my hand from the dagger-hilt and placed it on top of his bald head.

"No," I said. "No. Oh, no." But I said it in a slow whisper, because there was a strange dark justice in such a proposal, and genuine temptation as well. If I have never been much more in my life than a wandering mercenary of one sort or another, it has not been entirely out of laziness or uninterest. But most other possibilities had never endured beyond a drink and a daydream. Not once had I ever had to face the truth of what Master Caldrea had said of me: that I fled power because I desired it so much, because I feared my own ambition. I faced it now, in the eyes of the monks who had offered me their leadership—a mighty matter once again, with the Tree no longer draining the secret strength of *that place*—and also in my imagining of Lal's raised eyebrow and the fox's short, cold laugh if I should ever tell them of this moment. I said "No," once more, no louder, but differently, and walked past them to fetch my mare out of the stable.

No one moved or spoke until I had mounted and turned the mare's head toward the road. Then a younger monk, a shy man named Joshuo, "It could be different here. We could be different."

"No," I said, "you never could. But that is not my business, not at all. My business is to tell you that if anyone—*anyone*—from this place comes after me again, I will not only kill him, but I will return one last time and destroy this entire house, as I destroyed the Hunters' Tree. You know I can now."

And I rode away without a backward glance.

Somehow I managed to stay upright as far as the outskirts of a hamlet whose name I no longer recall, whereupon I toppled off my mare into an abandoned hayfield and slept for the remainder of the day, and most of the night. When I woke the stars were shockingly bright, I no longer seemed to be bleeding anywhere, and I was hardly limping at all. So I rode on, randomly heading due north, and why not? Northward lay the little kings, the smaller dukes, and the clan warlords, and one or another of them was bound to require a bodyguard, a caravan guide or a settler of their petty grudges, and all of these were things I knew how to do. For now and some little while to come, all directions, all pathways, all employments were going to feel very much the same.